ac-cept' \ik-'sept\ *verb*. take what is offered; agree or approve; believe something to be true.

al-low' \ə-'laü\ *verb*. make something possible; to provide for; permit to happen.

bal'ance \'ba-len(t)s\ *noun*. an instrument used for measuring objects; an amount that is owed; a harmonious state.

bene-fi'cial \,be-nə-'fi-shəl\ *adjective*. useful; fruitful; of value.

bril'liant \'bril-yənt\ *adjective*. bright; radiant; smart.

choose \'chüz\ *verb*. select; make a decision by rejecting other options.

col-lab-o-ra'tion \kə-,la-bə-'rā-shən\ *noun*. working with others to make something; the product of collaborating.

com-pas'sion \kəm-'pa-shən\ *noun*. sympathetic concern for others; pity for one's troubles.

con-sid'er-ate \kən-'si-d(ə-)rət\ *adjective*. someone who is careful not to hurt others.

cool \'kül\ *adjective*. a temperature that is more cold than hot; lacking excitement.

dif'fer-ent \'di-fərnt\ *adjective*. diverse things; not the same; unusual or distinct.

ex-pect' \ik-'spekt\ *verb*. to look forward to something that is likely to happen.

ex-press' \ik-'spres\ *verb*. convey a thought in words or by other means.

fire \'fī(-ə)r\ *noun*. combustion involving the combination of chemicals with oxygen, which gives out light and heat.

friend'ly \'fren(d)-lē\ *adjective*. related to being a friend; showing goodwill.

gen'er-ous \'jen-rəs\ *adjective*. showing kindness toward others; being willing to give to others.

har'mo-ny \'här-mə-nē\ *noun*. agreeing or pleasing combination of parts.

hu'man \'hyü-mən\ *noun*. a person; *Homo sapiens*.

in-clu'sive \in-'klü-siv\ *adjective*. covering a large scope or range of things.

in-spire' \in-'spī(-ə)r\ *verb*. to influence or guide, especially pertaining to creativity; to bring out.

joy \'jói\ *noun*. feeling of happiness; emotion evoked by success.

kind'ness \'kīn(d)-nəs\ *noun*. qualities of being helpful, sympathetic, loving, and affectionate.

know \'nō\ *verb*. perceive directly; be aware of the truth.

look \'lük\ *verb*. direct eyes toward something; use vision.

love \'ləv\ *noun*. intense feeling of affection.

men'tor \'men-,tór\ *noun*. a trusted counselor; a guide.

mil'lions \'mi(l)-yəns\ *noun*. a very large number.

mir'a-cles \'mir-i-kəls\ *noun*. surprising events not explicable by science; extraordinary events.

nav'i-gate \'na-və-,gāt\ *verb*. travel; follow a route.

neigh'bor-ly \'nā-bər-lē\ *adjective*. kind and helpful.

op'ti-mis-tic \'äp-tə-mist-ik\ *adjective*. describing a confident or hopeful person.

par'ty \'pär-tē\ *noun*. a gathering for socialization of invited guests, especially friends.

peace \'pēs\ *noun*. freedom from dispute; state of harmony.

pow'er \ ... noun. ability to make ... physica ...

quiet \ ... to no noise, silence.

re-source'ful \ri-'sórs-fəl\ *adjective*. cleverly finding solutions; overcoming problems and finding creative solutions.

sim'ple \'sim-pəl\ *adjective*. easy to understand; basic.

stel'lar \'ste-lər\ *adjective*. outstanding, relating to a performance.

strength \'streŋ(k)th\ *noun*. a state of being strong; ability to withstand a challenge.

ter-rif'ic \tə-'ri-fik\ *adjective*. excellent; really exciting.

to-geth'er \tə-'ge-thər\ *adverb*. with another person or people; a combination.

truth \'trüth\ *noun*. a state of being true; a fact.

un-der-stand'ing \ən-dər-'stan-diŋ\ *noun*. power of comprehending or mutual agreement between two or more people.

u-ni'ted \yu-'nī-təd\ *adjective*. brought together; usually for common beliefs or circumstances.

vo-cab'u-lar-y \vō-'ka-byə-,ler-ē\ *noun*. words used in language.

voice \'vóis\ *noun*. an opinion or personal expression.

warm'ing \'wórm-iŋ\ *adjective*. make or become warm.

word \'wərd\ *noun*. a single, yet powerful part of speech.

ya-hoo' \'yā-(,)hü\ *interjection*. a sound made out of excitement or happiness.

zone \'zōn\ *noun*. a specified area that serves a purpose; can be real or metaphorical.

A Peace Dragon-sized thank you to principal Letty Garcia, Ms. Rebore and Ms. Addeo's 2nd grade classes, and Mary G Clarkson Elementary for the words FRIENUNDERFUL and HONSPECTFUL!

Designed by Flowerpot Press
in Franklin, TN.
www.FlowerpotPress.com
Designer: Stephanie Meyers
Editor: Katrine Crow
DJS-0912-0164
ISBN: 978-1-4867-1210-6
Made in China/Fabriqué en Chine

Join us as we mix, mash, and make crazy, fun words to super inspire, absolutely encourage, and totally motivate each other.

Words, the first book in the Peace Dragon series, introduced the ability our words have to create compassionate conversations with ourselves and the world.

Alphabetter continues this thread with a playful take on empowering our vocabulary with hilarious words that encompass the best qualities, thoughts, and emotions we can imagine, in order to create a dictionary like no other. To further promote the power of our words, the bottom banner of each page takes impactful peace words and combines them to create ideas worth talking about. So start your word adventures, and see how they can change the world around you!

Always remember—your words matter.
Make them AMABULOUS!

♡ Linda

absomendous
{Absolutely + Tremendous}

amabulous
{Amazing + Fabulous}

astonding
{Astonishing + Outstanding}

Allept {Allow + Accept}
Allow yourself to be you, and accept that others are different.

BEBUD {Best + Buddy}

BEYAZING {Beyond + Amazing}

Balacoo {Balance + Cool}
Find your balance, and always remember to keep your cool.

Charvelous {Charming + Marvelous}

Cheviva {Cheery + Vivacious}

Clenious {Clever + Ingenious}

Choolo {Choose + Love}
Own your choices and their consequences,
and when given the choice, choose love.

DynaBuLouS
{Dynamic + Fabulous}

DaZZiDencE
{Dazzling + Confidence}

Diffether {Different + Together}
Always remember that our differences
work together.

EnTubeRant

{Entertaining + Exuberant}

EXTRiLLy

{Extra + Silly}

E e

Exprassion {Express + Compassion}
Express yourself through love, and always have compassion.

Fabulastic
{Fabulous + Fantastic}

Fabumendous
{Fabulous + Tremendous}

Frienunderful
{Friend + Fun + Wonderful}

Firarming {Fire + Warming}
Use your inner fire for warming others,
not burning them.

GOOLaRIOUS
{Goofy + Hilarious}

GREPFUL
{Great + Helpful}

Gg

Generindness {Generous + Kindness}
Be generous with your time, your smiles, and especially your kindness.

hERMiRaBLE

{Hero + Admirable}

honsPECTFuL

{Honest + Respectful}

Humunder {Human + Understand}
Love yourself and all other humans, too.
Understand we are all human.

inSPirEDIBLE

{Inspiring + Incredible}

Ii

Inspirmony {Inspire + Harmony}
Inspire harmony in the world around you and include everyone.

JOLLiGGLY

{Jolly + Giggly}

Jollaboration {Joy + Collaboration}
Joy is greater when shared, so joyfully collaborate with everyone.

Jj

Kinished {Kind + Cherished}

Knovigate {Know + Navigate}
If you know yourself, you can navigate any situation.

LEGEndaTiOnaL
{Legendary + Sensational}

LOVUGGabLe
{Loving + Huggable}

Looplete {Look + Complete}
Always look at the whole picture and get the complete story.

maJUMBLe
{Majestic + Humble}

maXCELLenT
{Magnificent + Excellent}

MiGhTERFUL
{Mighty + Powerful}

Menderate {Mentor + Considerate}
A mentor listens, holds you up, and keeps you going. Be a considerate mentor.

nivELouS {Nice + Marvelous}

Nn

Neighbendly {Neighborly + Friendly}
Being neighborly and friendly to people
will make them feel cherished.

OUTCEPTIONAL
{Outstanding + Exceptional}

OUTRASTIC
{Outrageous + Fantastic}

OUTSTOUNDING
{Outstanding + Astounding}

Optimific {Optimistic + Terrific}
Be an optimistic person who sees all
opportunities as terrific!

PhEnOmEnaTjOnaL

{Phenomenal + Inspirational}

PoWnOmEnaL

{Powerful + Phenomenal}

Powneficial {Power + Beneficial}
You have the power! Your power should be
beneficial to everyone around you.

QuiRuTie {Quirky + Cutie}

QuiveLy {Quite + Lovely}

Quilance {Quiet + Balance}
Peace can be found in the quiet. Tune into it, and find your balance.

RaDaZzLinG
{Radiant + Dazzling}

REMaPPy
{Remarkable + Happy}

Rr

Resillions {Resourceful + Millions}
Be resourceful. There are millions of ways to find and use your resources for good.

SPLENDICIOUS

{Splendid + Delicious}

SUPRONG

{Super + Strong}

Ss

Stelliant {Stellar + Brilliant}
Don't forget that you are stellar!
Always shine like a brilliant star!

TREMILLIANT
{Tremendously + Brilliant}

TRULACULAR
{Truly + Spectacular}

Trimple {Truth + Simple}
Be truthful. Truth is a simple, honorable path to follow.

Unbelarious
{Unbelievably + Hilarious}

Unbelunny
{Unbelievably + Funny}

Unitrength {United + Strength}
Strength comes when we stand together, united as one.

VEREET
{Very + Sweet}

VIVENDLY
{Vivacious + Friendly}

Voclusive {Voice + Inclusive}
We are better when we are inclusive.
Value every voice, especially your own!

WISHNATIVE

{Wishful + Imaginative}

WONABULOUS

{Wonderful + Fabulous}

Ww

Wokinabulary {Word + Kind + Vocabulary}
Build your kind word vocabulary, and share it with the world.

EXTRaMENDOUS
{Extraordinary + Tremendous}

eXperacles {Expect + Miracles}
Expect miracles, and notice them when they appear.

Yanificent {Yay + Magnificent}

Yippiful {Yippee + Beautiful}

Yumderful {Yummy + Wonderful}

Yy

Yaharty {Yahoo + Party}
Celebrate every day! Throw a party, do
what makes you happy, and shout YAHOO!

Zarific {Zany + Terrific}

Zeticulous {Zen + Fantastic + Fabulous}

Zz

Zeace {Zone + Peace}
Live in your zone. Live in peace. Live in the peace zone.

abs- am- asto-
che- cle- dyna-
fabu- fa- frie-
hermi- hon- inspi-
lovu- maju-
nivel- outcep-
pheno- po- quir-

bE-BEya-cha-
DazZ-EnTu-EXTRi-
GOO-GREP-
JoLLi-Kin-LeGEn-
MaXCE-Mi-
ouTRa-outs-
Qui-RaDa-REM-

SPLEN-SUP-TRE-
TRUL-UNBEL-UNBELU-
VER-VIVE-WISHNA-
WON-EXTRA-YAN-
YIPPI-YUM-
ZARI-
ZE!

ac-cept' \ik-'sept\ *verb.* take what is offered; agree or approve; believe something to be true.

al-low' \ə-'laù\ *verb.* make something possible; to provide for; permit to happen.

bal'ance \'ba-lən(t)s\ *noun.* an instrument used for measuring objects; an amount that is owed; a harmonious state.

bene-fi'cial \,be-nə-'fi-shəl\ *adjective.* useful; fruitful; of value.

bril'liant \'bril-yənt\ *adjective.* bright; radiant; smart.

choose \'chüz\ *verb.* select; make a decision by rejecting other options.

col-lab-o-ra'tion \kə-,la-bə-'rā-shən\ *noun.* working with others to make something; the product of collaborating.

com-pas'sion \kəm-'pa-shən\ *noun.* sympathetic concern for others; pity for one's troubles.

con-sid'er-ate \kən-'si-d(ə-)rət\ *adjective.* someone who is careful not to hurt others.

cool \'kül\ *adjective.* a temperature that is more cold than hot; lacking excitement.

dif'fer-ent \'di-fərnt\ *adjective.* diverse things; not the same; unusual or distinct.

ex-pect' \ik-'spekt\ *verb.* to look forward to something that is likely to happen.

ex-press' \ik-'spres\ *verb.* convey a thought in words or by other means.

fire \'fī(-ə)r\ *noun.* combustion involving the combination of chemicals with oxygen, which gives out light and heat.

friend'ly \'fren(d)-lē\ *adjective.* related to being a friend; showing goodwill.

gen'er-ous \'jen-rəs\ *adjective.* showing kindness toward others; being willing to give to others.

har'mo-ny \'här-mə-nē\ *noun.* agreeing or pleasing combination of parts.

hu'man \'hyü-mən\ *noun.* a person; Homo sapiens.

in-clu'sive \in-'klü-siv\ *adjective.* covering a large scope or range of things.

in-spire' \in-'spī(-ə)r\ *verb.* to influence or guide, especially pertaining to creativity; to bring out.

joy \'jòi\ *noun.* feeling of happiness; emotion evoked by success.

kind'ness \'kīn(d)-nəs\ *noun.* qualities of being helpful, sympathetic, loving, and affectionate.

know \'nō\ *verb.* perceive directly; be aware of the truth.

look \'lùk\ *verb.* direct eyes toward something; use vision.

love \'ləv\ *noun.* intense feeling of affection.

men'tor \'men-,tòr\ *noun.* a trusted counselor; a guide.

mil'lions \'mi(l)-yəns\ *noun.* a very large number.

mir'a-cles \'mir-i-kəls\ *noun.* surprising events not explicable by science; extraordinary events.

nav'i-gate \'na-və-,gāt\ *verb.* travel; follow a route.

neigh'bor-ly \'nā-bər-lē\ *adjective.* kind and helpful.

op'ti-mis-tic \'äp-tə-mist-ik\ *adjective.* describing a confident or hopeful person.

par'ty \'pär-tē\ *noun.* a gathering for socialization of invited guests, especially friends.

peace \'pēs\ *noun.* freedom from dispute; state of harmony.

pow'er \'paù(-ə)r\ *noun.* ability to make something happen; physical ability.

quiet \'kwī-ət\ *adjective.* with little to no noise; without interruption; silence.

re-source'ful \ri-'sòrs-fəl\ *adjective.* cleverly finding solutions; overcoming problems and finding creative solutions.

sim'ple \'sim-pəl\ *adjective.* easy to understand; basic.

stel'lar \'ste-lər\ *adjective.* outstanding, relating to a performance.

strength \'stren(k)th\ *noun.* a state of being strong; ability to withstand a challenge.

ter-rif'ic \tə-'ri-fik\ *adjective.* excellent; really exciting.

to-geth'er \tə-'ge-thər\ *adverb.* with another person or people; a combination.

truth \'trüth\ *noun.* a state of being true; a fact.

un-der-stand'ing \ən-dər-'stan-diŋ\ *noun.* power of comprehending or mutual agreement between two or more people.

u-ni'ted \yù-'nī-ted\ *adjective.* brought together; usually for common beliefs or circumstances.

vo-cab'u-lar-y \vō-'ka-byə-,ler-ē\ *noun.* words used in language.

voice \'vòis\ *noun.* an opinion or personal expression.

warm'ing \'wòrm-iŋ\ *adjective.* make or become warm.

word \'wərd\ *noun.* a single, yet powerful part of speech.

ya-hoo' \'yä-(,)hü\ *interjection.* a sound made out of excitement or happiness.

zone \'zōn\ *noun.* a specified area that serves a purpose; can be real or metaphorical.

ac-cept' \ik-'sept\ *verb.* take what is offered; agree or approve; believe something to be true.

al-low' \ə-'lau̇\ *verb.* make something possible; to provide for; permit to happen.

bal'ance \'ba-lən(t)s\ *noun.* an instrument used for measuring objects; an amount that is owed; a harmonious state.

bene-fi'cial \ˌbe-nə-'fi-shəl\ *adjective.* useful; fruitful; of value.

bril'liant \'bril-yənt\ *adjective.* bright; radiant; smart.

choose \'chüz\ *verb.* select; make a decision by rejecting other options.

col-lab-o-ra'tion \kə-ˌla-bə-'rā-shən\ *noun.* working with others to make something; the product of collaborating.

com-pas'sion \kəm-'pa-shən\ *noun.* sympathetic concern for others; pity for one's troubles.

con-sid'er-ate \kən-'si-d(ə-)rət\ *adjective.* someone who is careful not to hurt others.

cool \'kül\ *adjective.* a temperature that is more cold than hot; lacking excitement.

dif'fer-ent \'di-fərnt\ *adjective.* diverse things; not the same; unusual or distinct.

ex-pect' \ik-'spekt\ *verb.* to look forward to something that is likely to happen.

ex-press' \ik-'spres\ *verb.* convey a thought in words or by other means.

fire \'fī(-ə)r\ *noun.* combustion involving the combination of chemicals with oxygen, which gives out light and heat.

friend'ly \'fren(d)-lē\ *adjective.* related to being a friend; showing goodwill.

gen'er-ous \'jen-rəs\ *adjective.* showing kindness toward others; being willing to give to others.

har'mo-ny \'här-mə-nē\ *noun.* agreeing or pleasing combination of parts.

hu'man \'hyü-mən\ *noun.* a person; *Homo sapiens*.

in-clu'sive \in-'klü-siv\ *adjective.* covering a large scope or range of things.

in-spire' \in-'spī(-ə)r\ *verb.* to influence or guide, especially pertaining to creativity; to bring out.

joy \'jȯi\ *noun.* feeling of happiness; emotion evoked by success.

kind'ness \'kīn(d)-nəs\ *noun.* qualities of being helpful, sympathetic, loving, and affectionate.

know \'nō\ *verb.* perceive directly; be aware of the truth.

look \'lu̇k\ *verb.* direct eyes toward something; use vision.

love \'ləv\ *noun.* intense feeling of affection.

men'tor \'men-ˌtȯr\ *noun.* a trusted counselor; a guide.

mil'lions \'mi(l)-yəns\ *noun.* a very large number.

mir'a-cles \'mir-i-kəls\ *noun.* surprising events not explicable by science; extraordinary events.

nav'i-gate \'na-və-ˌgāt\ *verb.* travel; follow a route.

neigh'bor-ly \'nā-bər-lē\ *adjective.* kind and helpful.

op'ti-mis-tic \'äp-tə-mist-ik\ *adjective.* describing a confident or hopeful person.

par'ty \'pär-tē\ *noun.* a gathering for socialization of invited guests, especially friends.

peace \'pēs\ *noun.* freedom from dispute; state of harmony.

pow'er \'pau̇(-ə)r\ *noun.* ability to make something happen; physical ability.

quiet \'kwī-ət\ *adjective.* with little to no noise; without interruption; silence.

re-source'ful \ri-'sȯrs-fəl\ *adjective.* cleverly finding solutions; overcoming problems and finding creative solutions.

sim'ple \'sim-pəl\ *adjective.* easy to understand; basic.

stel'lar \'ste-lər\ *adjective.* outstanding, relating to a performance.

strength \'stren(k)th\ *noun.* a state of being strong; ability to withstand a challenge.

ter-rif'ic \tə-'ri-fik\ *adjective.* excellent; really exciting.

to-geth'er \tə-'ge-thər\ *adverb.* with another person or people; a combination.

truth \'trüth\ *noun.* a state of being true; a fact.

un-der-stand'ing \ən-dər-'stan-diŋ\ *noun.* power of comprehending or mutual agreement between two or more people.

u-ni'ted \yu̇-'nī-təd\ *adjective.* brought together; usually for common beliefs or circumstances.

vo-cab'u-lar-y \vō-'ka-byə-ˌler-ē\ *noun.* words used in language.

voice \'vȯis\ *noun.* an opinion or personal expression.

warm'ing \'wȯrm-iŋ\ *adjective.* make or become warm.

word \'wərd\ *noun.* a single, yet powerful part of speech.

ya-hoo' \'yä-(ˌ)hü\ *interjection.* a sound made out of excitement or happiness.

zone \'zōn\ *noun.* a specified area that serves a purpose; can be real or metaphorical.